Disney KINGDOMS
SEEKERS OF THE WEIRD
#4

When their parents were kidnapped by Despoina and the sinister Shadow Society, Maxwell and Melody Keep followed their mysterious Uncle Roland through a portal to the Museum of the Weird, a vast depository of the world's most powerful—and threatening—supernatural objects.

To ensure the safety of the elder Keeps, Despoina demanded the Coffin Clock be turned over to her by the time the Candleman burned down. With Roland injured, the Keep siblings assumed the task of locating the pieces of the Living Room—magical furniture scattered throughout the museum that, once collected, would summon the Clock.

The museum's Head Warden tried to stop the kids, warning them that the Coffin Clock was actually a prison for the Reaper King, and that Despoina planned to unleash him and doom the world. Maxwell and Melody, not willing to sacrifice their parents, refused to give up their quest. With the help of the Mushroom People and a magical amulet they found in the museum, they escaped the Wardens and retreated to Roland, who equipped the kids with new weapons to help them survive the museum...

| MAXWELL KEEP Brother | MELODY KEEP Sister | ROLAND KEEP Uncle, Warden | CANDLEMAN Timekeeper | EFRAIN FENTON WHETSTONE Uncle, Warden | DESPOINA Leader of the Shadow Society |

BRANDON SEIFERT writer   KARL MOLINE penciler   RICK MAGYAR inker

JEAN-FRANCOIS BEAULIEU colorist   VC'S JOE CARAMAGNA letterer

MICHAEL DEL MUNDO cover artist   BRIAN CROSBY variant cover artist

JIM CLARK, BRIAN CROSBY, TOM MORRIS & JOSH SHIPLEY walt disney imagineers

MARK BASSO assistant editor   BILL ROSEMANN editor

AXEL ALONSO editor in chief   JOE QUESADA chief creative officer   DAN BUCKLEY publisher

special thanks to DAVID GABRIEL

MUSEUM OF THE WEIRD inspired by the designs of ROLLY CRUMP

Spotlight

MARVEL
marvelkids.com

ABDOPUBLISHING.COM

Reinforced library bound edition published in 2017 by Spotlight,
a division of ABDO, PO Box 398166, Minneapolis, Minnesota 55439.
Spotlight produces high-quality reinforced library bound editions for
schools and libraries. Published by agreement with Marvel Characters, Inc.

Printed in the United States of America, North Mankato, Minnesota.
042016
092016

 marvelkids.com
© 2014 MARVEL

Elements based on
Walt Disney's
Museum of the Weird
© Disney.

PUBLISHER'S CATALOGING IN PUBLICATION DATA

Names: Seifert, Brandon, author. | Moline, Karl ; Magyar, Rick ; Beaulieu, Jean-Francois ;
    Andrade, Filipe, illustrators.
Title: Disney Kingdoms : Seekers of the weird / by Brandon Seifert ; illustrated by Karl Moline,
    Rick Magyar, Jean-Francois Beaulieu, and Filipe Andrade.
Description: Minneapolis, MN : Spotlight, [2017] | Series: Disney Kingdoms : seekers of the
    weird
Summary: When their parents are abducted, Melody and Maxwell Keep follow their estranged
    uncle Roland through a portal to the Museum of the Weird, and are thrust into a dangerous
    mission to save their family and the world from an evil shadow society!
Identifiers: LCCN 2016932365 | ISBN 9781614795148 (v.1 : lib. bdg.) | ISBN 9781614795155
    (v. 2 : lib. bdg.) | ISBN 9781614795162 (v. 3 : lib. bdg.) | ISBN 9781614795179 (v. 4 : lib.
    bdg.) | ISBN 9781614795186 (v. 5 : lib. bdg.)
Subjects: LCSH: Disney (Fictitious characters)--Juvenile fiction. | Rescues--Juvenile fiction. |
    Museums--Juvenile fiction. | Adventure and adventurers--Juvenile fiction. | Comic books,
    strips, etc.--Juvenile fiction. | Graphic novels--Juvenile fiction.
Classification: DDC 741.5--dc23
LC record available at http://lccn.loc.gov/2016932365

ABDO

Spotlight

A Division of ABDO
abdopublishing.com

THE MUSEUM OF THE WEIRD.
DAY SEVEN.

LOOK ON THE **BRIGHT SIDE!** WE FINALLY FOUND THE **LAST PIECE** OF THE LIVING ROOM!

≶OOPH≶

NOW WE JUST HAVE TO GET IT **BACK.**

WITHOUT, YOU KNOW, **DYING TOO MUCH.**

SO? HOW WE **DOING,** MELODY?

THEY **STILL OUT** THERE?

DUMB QUESTION.

OF **COURSE** THE MAN-EATING PLANTS ARE **STILL OUTSIDE,** MAXWELL.

THIS IS WHERE THEY **LIVE.**

TOP FLOOR OF THE MUSEUM. THE HOTHOUSE.

YOU READY FOR MORE "PRACTICE" WITH OUR **NEW WEAPONS?**

READY? FOR **CALISTHENICS?** NEVER.

THAT COULD HAVE GONE BETTER.

I'M SO SICK OF THIS GARDEN SHED.

HEY! THIS *IS* A GARDEN SHED!

THAT MEANS IT'S FULL OF *TOOLS!* FOR GARDENING!

MAYBE I CAN FIND THE "*TAMING POTION*" FOR THE PLANTS! REMEMBER *UNCLE ROLAND* MENTIONING IT?

MAXWELL! THE *EVIL PLANTS* ARE GOING TO GET IN!

WOULD YOU *GET BACK HERE* ALREADY?

OH, HEY!

ROLAND'S GUN! HE MUST HAVE *DROPPED* IT. THIS MUST BE WHERE HE...UH... WHERE HIS *LEGS* GOT HURT.

GIVE IT HERE!

EW.

SHLURP

"THOUGHT YOU'D *NEVER* GET BACK."

CANDLEMAN'S ALMOST BURNED DOWN.

OUT OF *TIME.*

THE LIVING QUARTERS.

GLAD YOU FOUND MY *ST. LOUIS SPECIALS,* THOUGH.

ROLAND *MISSED YOU,* LADIES.

EW, AGAIN.

UNCLE ROLAND, HOW IS *ARRANGING SOME FURNITURE* GOING TO BRING BACK THE *COFFIN CLOCK?*

ONCE ASSEMBLED-- *PROPERLY--*THE LIVING ROOM INTONES THE *CONJURATION.*

TO SUMMON THE COFFIN CLOCK OUT OF THE *"CRAWLWAY,"* THE *SPACE BETWEEN.*

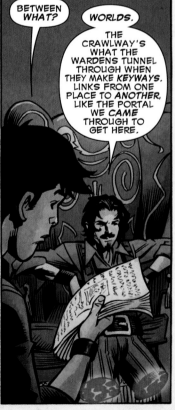

BETWEEN *WHAT?*

WORLDS.

THE CRAWLWAY'S WHAT THE WARDENS TUNNEL THROUGH WHEN THEY MAKE *KEYWAYS.* LINKS FROM ONE PLACE TO *ANOTHER,* LIKE THE PORTAL WE *CAME* THROUGH TO GET HERE.

COFFIN CLOCK'S HIDDEN IN THE *SPACE BETWEEN SPACES.* INSIDE THE CLOCK, THE REAPER KING'S TRAPPED IN THE *MOMENT BETWEEN MOMENTS.*

ALL *QUITE* POETIC.

WAS THE CONJURATION... SUPPOSED TO HAVE *STARTED* YET?

AH. THE CONJURATION IS SELF-POWERED--BUT NEEDS A "*SPARK*" TO START IT. LIKE AN AUTOMOBILE IGNITION.

"*PAIN*"? ISN'T THAT WHAT THIS *ENTIRE WEEK* HAS BEEN?

IT NEEDS... "A SACRIFICE OF *PAIN.*"

WE HAVE TO HURT OURSELVES? YOU NEVER MENTIONED THAT!

DOESN'T HAVE TO BE *MUCH* PAIN. JUST *SOME,* WHILE IN CONTACT WITH A *FURNITURE PIECE.*

OW.

IT'S *WORKING* ALREADY?

BUT YOU DIDN'T SACRIFICE ANY *PAIN,* UNCLE--

--OH. SORRY.

WHAT'S *NEXT?*

AT THE *END* OF THE CONJURATION, THE CLOCK WILL FALL OUT OF THE CRAWLWAY...

BY *YOUR FATHER'S BROTHER.*

"OBVIOUSLY"-- AS *HE* WOULD SAY.

I...I CAN'T BELIEVE IT! *ROLAND?* THE WARDENS WERE *RIGHT?*

YOU *WERE* WORKING WITH THE SOCIETY THE *WHOLE* TIME? THE *WHOLE* TIME? EVEN THOUGH THEY KIDNAPPED OUR--

KIDS!

DAD!

MOMMY!

AT LAST, THE FAMILY *REUNITED!*

OR THEY *WILL BE,* ONCE YOU TURN OVER THE *COFFIN CLOCK* TO US. PER OUR... *"AGREEMENT."*

AND LET US NOT DO ANYTHING *FOOLISH,* SHALL WE?

GET HER!

NO! STOP!

KRAK

CHILDREN. ⟩TSK⟨ ⟩TSK⟨

ROLAND DIDN'T TATTLE?

SHRIPP

ABOUT OUR *GRAND* DESTINY?

SLASSH

I *DID* TELL YOU.

DESPOINA AND THE SOCIETY ARE CLAD IN THEIR *SHADOWS.* THEY CAN'T BE HARMED.

EXCEPT UNDER VERY RARE CIRCUMSTANCES...

SHADOWS MAKE EXCELLENT *ARMOR. MORTALITY* CAN'T PIERCE THEM.

ONE REALLY SHOULDN'T LEAVE THEM *DRAGGING AROUND* BEHIND ONESELF.

NOW, THEN...

...WE HAVE WAITED CENTURIES TOO LONG ALREADY, CHILDREN.

WE KNOW THE KEYS TO THE COFFIN CLOCK ARE IN YOUR POSSESSION, AND THAT ONLY *YOU* ARE FATED TO USE THEM.

PLEASE, PRAY YOU WIND THE CLOCK...SO WE ARE NOT FORCED TO SMITE YOUR PARENTS.

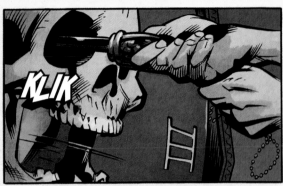

KLIK

TICK TICK TICK

THAT'S ALL? WHAT ABOUT THE *REAPER KING?*

INDEED. WHERE IS MY *LOST LOVE,* ROLAND?

...WHEN THE CLOCK STRIKES THE *TWELFTH HOUR.*

THAT'S WHEN THE *REAPER KING* WILL BE *LOOSED* UPON THE WORLD AGAIN.

SPLENDID RESEARCH!

HERE ARE THE *THREE MILLION* PIECES OF SILVER WE *PROMISED YOU* FOR YOUR SERVICES.

TELL US, THOUGH. HOW DOES ONE *FEEL* AFTER STABBING EVERY BACK THAT EVER TRUSTED YOU?

IN TRUTH?

IT WAS *MUCH HARDER* THAN I THOUGHT...

...TO MAINTAIN MY *ILLUSION OF BETRAYAL* LONG ENOUGH TO SECURE YOU IN MY *TRAP.*

ROLAND?

WHAT *INTERESTING TWIST* DO YOU HAVE FOR US *THIS TIME?*

I CALLED THE CAVALRY.

OBVIOUSLY.

THE WARDENS?!

ROLAND, YOU *SCUM*. YOU *STEAL* OUR KEYS TO THE MUSEUM. THEN YOU *TELEPORT* THEM BACK TO US.

ALLOWING US TO ARRIVE JUST IN TIME...TO CATCH DESPOINA PAYING YOU FOR *BETRAYING* US!

YOU'RE LATE, WHETSTONE. CLOCK'S ALREADY TICKING.

LADIES AND GENTLEMEN... YOU'VE ALL BEEN *HAD*.

THE CLOCK, THE WARDENS' KEYS, MY "ALLIANCE" WITH *DESPOINA*? ALL A *CLEVER PLOT* DEVISED BY MY *BROTHER*, SISTER-IN-LAW, AND *YOURS TRULY*...TO LURE THE SOCIETY HERE.

SO WE CAN *DESTROY THEM* FOREVA*GGGGGH!*

WHETSTONE! WHAT ARE YOU--

YOU KNOW OUR LAWS, ROLAND.

YOU HAVE *BETRAYED US* TO THE ENEMY. YOU ARE A TRAITOR TO THE *CAUSE*--AND TO *HUMANITY.*

AND TO ATTEMPT *IMPLICATING* YOUR *BLOOD RELATIVES?* YOU'RE WORSE THAN *DESPOINA.*

YOU KNOW OUR PUNISHMENT FOR TRAITORS.

WAIT! I'M *NOT* A TRAITOR! THIS WAS A *STING!* TO GET THE SOCIETY INTO THE MUSEUM, SO WE CAN *DESTROY* THEM!

ARTHUR AND ELLEN WILL *VOUCH* FOR ME!

ARTHUR? ELLEN?

EXECRATIONS.

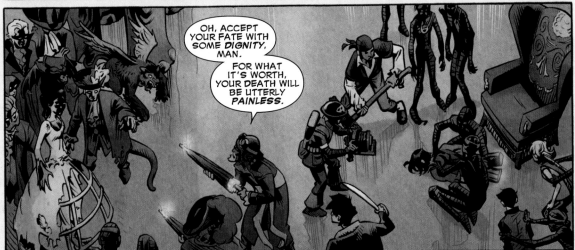

OH, ACCEPT YOUR FATE WITH SOME *DIGNITY,* MAN.

FOR WHAT IT'S WORTH, YOUR DEATH WILL BE UTTERLY *PAINLESS.*

TRAITOR! *SNAKE!*

STUPID, STUPID LEGS. STUPID...

...STUPID EVERYTHING.

KIDS!

REMEMBER *LAST TIME* HUSKS FOUGHT TAXIDERMA?

GIDDY UP!

ROLAND! BETRAYER AND COWARD! *FACE YOUR FATE!*

HE WON'T GET *FAR!* I'LL TAKE A SQUAD--

NO, KINSLEY. WE STOP THE SOCIETY-- OR THE *WORLD'S* FORFEIT.

IT PAINS ME TO LET THE DIRTY TRAITOR LIVE, EVEN FOR ANOTHER HOUR...

..BUT WHAT MORE CAN AN INVALID AND TWO CHILDREN DO WHEN THEY'VE ALREADY DOOMED THE WORLD?

TO BE CONCLUDED!

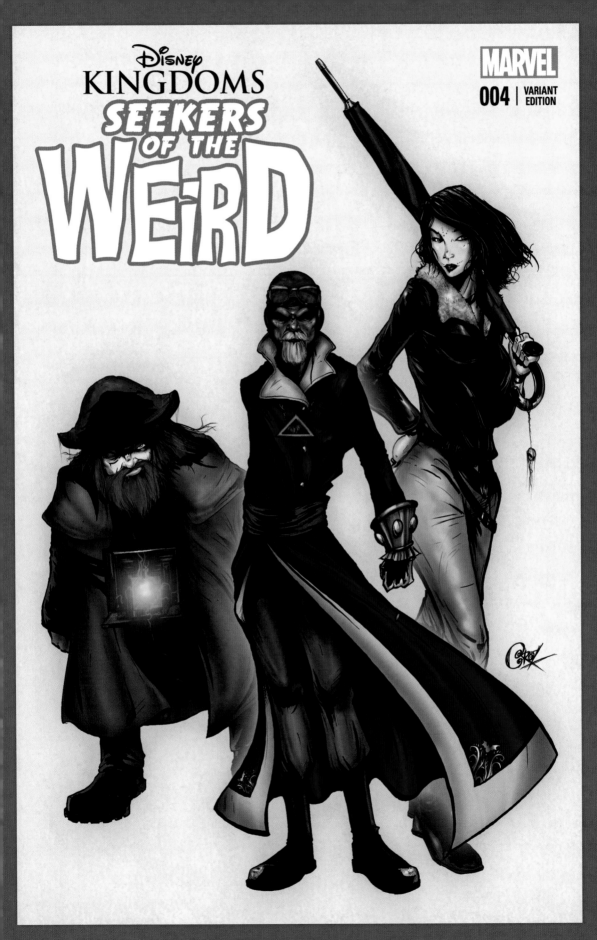

Disney Kingdoms: Seekers of the Weird #4 — Variant Cover by Brian Crosby

COLLECT THEM ALL!

Set of 5 Hardcover Books ISBN: 978-1-61479-513-1

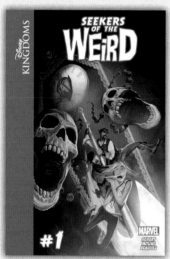

Hardcover Book ISBN
978-1-61479-514-8

Hardcover Book ISBN
978-1-61479-515-5

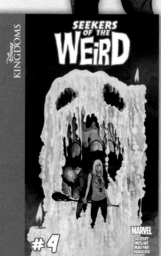

Hardcover Book ISBN
978-1-61479-516-2

Hardcover Book ISBN
978-1-61479-517-9

Hardcover Book ISBN
978-1-61479-518-6